AstroBall
Free-4-All

Books by Robert Elmer

AstroKids

Promise of Zion

Adventures Down Under

The Young Underground

ROBERT ELMER

AstroKids

AstroBall
Free-4-All

BETHANY BACKYARD®

www.bethanyhouse.com

AstroBall Free-4-All
Copyright © 2002
Robert Elmer

Cover and text illustrations by Paul Turnbaugh
Cover design by Lookout Design Group, Inc.

Unless otherwise identified, Scripture quotations are from the *International Children's Bible, New Century Version,* copyright © 1986, 1988 by W Publishing Group, Nashville, Tennessee. Used by permission.

Published by Bethany House Publishers
A Ministry of Bethany Fellowship International
11400 Hampshire Avenue South
Bloomington, Minnesota 55438
www.bethanyhouse.com

Printed in the United States of America by
Bethany Press International, Bloomington, Minnesota 55438

Library of Congress Cataloging-in-Publication Data

Elmer, Robert.
    Astroball free-4-all / by Robert Elmer.
      p. cm. — (Astrokids ; 8)
Summary: Mir's father has pulled strings to have him named captain of the *CLEO-7* Astroball team just before the big tournament, and Mir, who knows little about the game, is tempted to cheat rather than lose. Includes facts about robots and instructions for decoding a secret message.
    ISBN 0-7642-2628-2 (pbk.)
    [1. Ball games—Fiction. 2. Contests—Fiction. 3. Sportsmanship—Fiction. 4. Space stations—Fiction. 5. Christian life—Fiction. 6. Science fiction.]
I. Title.
    PZ7. E4794 As   2002
    [Fic]—dc21   2002001343

To the Bond family—

Dirk, Julia, and kids.

Robert

Freckles

ROBERT ELMER is an Earth-based space correspondent who writes for life-forms all over the solar system. He and his family live about ninety-three million miles from the sun with their dog, Freckles. Like Zero-G, Freckles likes to chase all kinds of balls (even astroballs, if she could find one), but don't ask her to fetch. She just runs away with the ball, laughing her doggy-laugh. Go, Freckles!

Contents

✳ ✳ ✳

MEET THE
AstroKids

Lamar "Buzz" Bright

Show the way, Buzz! The leader of the AstroKids always has a great plan. He also loves Jupiter ice cream.

Daphne "DeeBee" Ortiz

DeeBee's the brains of the bunch—she can build or fix almost anything. But, suffering satellites, don't tell her she's a "GEEN-ius"!

Theodore "Tag" Ortiz

Yeah, DeeBee's little brother, Tag, always tags along. Count on him to say something silly at just the wrong time. He's in orbit.

Kumiko "Miko" Sato

Everybody likes Miko the stowaway. They just don't know how she got to be a karate master, or how she knows so much about space shuttles.

Vladimir "Mir" Chekhov

So his dad's the station commander and Mir usually gets his way? Give him a break! He's trying. And whatever he did, it was probably just a joke.

Take Me Out to the Tryouts

* * *

Take me out to the astroball game,
Wire me up to the e-reader hyperport.
Buy me some space nuts and Jupiter-jack,
I don't care if I never get back.
Let me root, root, root for the AstroKids,
If they don't win, it's a shame.
For it's 01, 02, 03 hyperstrikes, you're out
At the astroball game!
   —"No Fear" Mir Chekhov
      (with apologies to Jack Norworth)

Pretty catchy song, huh?

I don't want to brag. *Nyet,* no way. But I wrote it.

Okay, okay. Maybe you've heard something like it before. But that was the old baseball version back on Earth, way back when. My new song is for astroball, which is what we play up here on *CLEO*-7. After all, it's 2175, and . . . What's that?

"Strike one!"

The floating drone-ump squawked and pointed. He looked kind of like a floating silver watermelon, except for his three extend-o eyes and three arms.

Who wrote that drone-ump's program? I thought. *If that was a hyperstrike, then—*

"Wake up, Mir!" My friend Buzz yelled at me from behind the tryout line. "Keep your eye on the ball."

"I am!" I looked back at the silver ball that had just plunked into the catcher's mitt with a *fwuump!*

I could have hit it. If I'd wanted to.

"You can do it!" Easy for Buzz to say. He wasn't staring down the solar system's fastest pitcher-drone. The drone even had a laser guidance system. DeeBee told me this one was good for throwing balls up to 103 kilometers per hour.

That's fast, by the way.

Trust me.

"Choke up on the bat!" Buzz yelled.

"Nyet! I'm not going to choke!"

Come to think of it, my throat *did* feel kind of tight. In fact . . .

Gag!

More air!

Gasp!

"Strike two!" yelled the drone-ump.

I tried to take a couple of deep-space survivor breaths. But they only made my head spin.

Now I was in trouble. *Big* trouble. I looked around, but everything was a big blur. I could hear the roar of the crowd, like a Saturn 88 rocket lifting off.

Of course, with my luck, I would be left standing right underneath, getting a big-time burn.

Knock it off! I told myself. *Don't let anybody see you choke. It's only a tryout.*

Yeah, only a tryout for the biggest games of my life—the All-*CLEO* AstroBall Tournament. You know, *CLEO-7* against *CLEO-5*, or *CLEO-2* against *CLEO-4*, and so on. May the best space station win.

This was serious stuff. Sink or swim. Do or die. Honor and glory and prizes.

That's what I was thinking when I peeked up at the double-sized 3-D hologram of the solar system's most famous professional astroball coach.

Tommy LaSolar.

"You ready for another pitch, son?" he asked me.

Gulp.

Now, get this: Coach LaSolar was really in his *CLEO*-sport office on the moon colony. A 3-D holo-vid projector near the ceiling of the rec-pod made it so he could see and talk to us just like he was really here.

QUESTION 01:

Hold it. Rec-pod? No one has ever said anything about a rec-pod before.

ANSWER 01:

It's all new! "Rec" stands for recreation, as in games and stuff. And the "pod" is a huge, triple-sized space-gym they hooked up to the outside of the station last month. You should see it: three diamond-shaped playing fields marked off with red and green laser beams, plus a springy floor and a tall ceiling. Four drone-umps float above each field, and there are six replay screens. Very cool!

"Son? Are you ready?"

I wasn't Tommy LaSolar's son. He called everybody that, maybe because he was the chief coach for all the *CLEO* stations.

He looked down his nose at me, squinted, and chewed his big wad of official major league AstroBall Bubblegum.

And he was still waiting for an answer.

"Pitch away." I dug my gripper shoes into the Astroturf and tried not to float away.

"You can do it, Mir!" That was my mom, from the floating bleachers on the sidelines. Ask her if we were playing astroball or basketball or Ping-Pong. I don't think she'd know the difference.

I wiped the sweat from my forehead with the back of my hand and squeezed the round handle of my flat bat a little more tightly.

Here goes, I thought. I was ready. I had watched my e-reader lesson twenty-two gazillion

times—when nobody else was looking. "Astroball
in 12 Easy Steps," starring Mister e.

QUESTION 02:
Who is Mister e?
ANSWER 02:
Mister e is the digital instructor on the e-
reader. You know, like a cartoon character.
He explains things like how to play Martian
triple chess, or how to hit a home run in
astroball. Any game you want to know,
Mister e can demo for you.

I called a quick time out and sneaked a peek at
the reader in my pocket one more time. I watched
Mister e do the step-by-step replay. Here goes:

Step 01: All right, kids, keep your eye on the ball.
(You bet.)
Step 02: Bat off the shoulder. (I'm there.)
Step 03: Step into the pitch with the left foot. (Got it.)
Step 04: Easy, level swing. (Check.)

"Play ball!" buzzed the drone-ump.

I slipped Mister e back into my pocket.

The pitcher-drone wound up one more time.

I counted off the rest of the steps in my head.

Step 05: Connect for a big hit. (No problem.)

Step 06: Impress Coach LaSolar and make the team. (Well, sure!)

Now here came the *real* ball, a silver streak.

Whoooosh!

Astrodogs With
2 Extra Marstard ✳ ✳ ✳

"Steeee-rrrrike THREE!" yelled the drone-ump.

Did he have to pump his arms and do a three-handed strikeout wave? Everyone already knew I'd missed the ball. Besides . . .

"The sun was in my eyes!" I pointed up at the skylight. A little ray of starshine peeked through from behind the big, round dish of the moon. Hey, if you saw it, you'd say the same thing. I mean, how could I hit a high-speed astroball when the light was right smack-dab in my eyes?

Well, it was pretty close, anyway.

Or it could have been.

At least, it *should* have been.

"All right, 5702. Next batter." Coach LaSolar pointed at the line of kids behind me.

Yeah, next batter. Number 5702—me—had struck out.

But with style.

"That's okay, Mir." Buzz slapped me on the back. "You'll show him how fast you can run. Or how well you can pitch, right? Just wait."

Whatever. I headed back to the stands and tried to slip into the crowd. But I couldn't even do *that*.

"Wonderfool, Mir!" That would be my mom, Mrs. Chekhov. "You svungk your bat beautiful. So strong, my Mir! I hear the air move when you svungk. The coach, he liked that, no?"

"Nyet, I don't think so, Mom. I missed."

"Of course you missed. But that was just to show strong svingk, nyet?"

I sighed and tried to duck away from her mussing up my hair. How did she manage that even when I was wearing my hat?

Just between you and me, I didn't know how to play astroball so well. I had played lots of soccer back in Russia, before we moved up here to the station, but never astroball.

Still, thanks to Mister e, I knew more about

astroball than my mom. And that was enough to know Coach LaSolar wasn't ready to sign Mir Chekhov to a pro contract.

Not just yet.

QUESTION 03:

Strikes, bats, coaches, umps . . . All this sounds a lot like baseball, doesn't it?

ANSWER 03:

Yes, but astroball's different. The astrobat is flat, except for the handle, and the ball has a spinning gyro top inside. When you hit it, the ball goes straight, then bounces all over the place. Pretty crazy. Of course, that's also because we play in less than a quarter G.

QUESTION 04:

A quarter G? Is that some kind of musical note, like B flat minor?

ANSWER 04:

Nope. A quarter G means there's hardly any gravity. Things are almost weightless, but not quite. It makes it easy to jump really high—and to forget which way is up.

CRAAACK!

Back at the tryouts, everybody cheered as Buzz hit another one. The astroball bounced first against the side wall . . .

Boinnng!

. . . then off the ceiling.

Bwaaang!

More cheers. Buzz thwacked another one to the far corner.

Well, at least *somebody* knew how to hit. Me, I was going to be lucky to make the team.

But I just *had* to. I had to show Mom I could do it. And I had to show Dad . . .

I looked up just long enough to see the seat beside my mom was still empty. Not that I was surprised. But I had been hoping that even the station commander could take a few minutes off.

"Is Dad—?"

"He will be here soon," my mom told me. "He had important meetingk."

Sure. My dad always had *important meetingks* from here clear to Venus.

"After tryouts, he will take you to get Jupiter ice cream. My champion needs to eat, nyet?"

Well, sure. Maybe I wouldn't strike out so much with a little astroball park food in my stomach.

Mmm, yeah. I could already smell it. Somebody had even programmed the food drones with loud ballpark voices:

"ASTROdogs, get your dogs HERE-ah!"

I just need a little more muscle, I told myself. A couple astrodogs with extra yellow marstard and Pluto relish should do the trick. I had just loaded up when I heard my number again.

"5702, you're next to run. Get set."

Now, *this* I could do. But showing my speed with an astrodog in each hand wouldn't be too classy. So I took a big bite and gently stuffed them inside my blue-and-red jersey to keep them safe. And then I took off.

Yeah! Mir Chekhov, human space probe. Refueled and ready to launch! Coach LaSolar would forget my strikeout when he saw how fast I

could move. I pumped my legs and beelined for the base.

WHOOSHKY! You should have seen me move. Faster than a speeding cosmonaut.

"Now slide!" ordered Coach LaSolar. "Down!"

Yeah, I'd seen this on Mister e's "Astroball in 12 Easy Steps."

Step 01: Run with your head down. (No problem.)
Step 02: Put your arms out about two meters from the base. (Okay.)
Step 03: Slide headfirst. (Here I come!)

People said later I ran really well. And I think I made a pretty good slide, too. Headfirst, even.

It's just that I forgot about the two astrodogs parked inside my shirt. You know. The ones with

3 Roster Check ✳ ✳ ✳

Ever smashed two astrodogs with extra mar-stard inside your brand-new sports jersey? I didn't think so. I didn't see why people thought it was so funny.

"Do that again, Mir!" Tag was rolling.

Me, I just drifted off to change my jersey, and quick.

Pretty soon it would be time for Coach La-Solar to tell us the list of players who had made the team. He was going to read us the roster for the first time.

"Stand by," said Coach LaSolar. "I'll be back to you with the roster in a micro-second."

Maybe he was thinking about it. I could understand that. But three minutes went by, then five. And the rec-pod was so quiet you could have heard a partial eclipse of the moon.

(I know. Eclipses don't make noise. When the moon gets a big shadow on it, that's an eclipse. But that's the point! Eclipses are *quiet*.)

"My agent's probably asking for more money," Tag told us. "I'm holding out for twenty million and chocolate Jupiter ice cream at every home game."

"Chocolate? That's all?" I tossed an astroball in the air.

While we're waiting, maybe it's time for . . .

Mir Chekhov's Very Unofficial AstroPlayers Roster

(Remember, this isn't the real team—yet.)

"LADIES AND GENTLEPEOPLE, AT FIRST BASE, NUMBER FORTY-SEVEN, BUUUUZZ BRIGHT!"

Buzz is a natural. Can you say "star"? And I don't mean, like, Andromeda 7. He does everything better than all the rest of us put together. At least, for now. I'm working on catching up.

"BEHIND THE PLATE CATCHING,

YOUR GENIUS AND MINE, DEEBEEEE ORTIZ!"

DeeBee can catch pretty well. But she's too busy thinking about her new experiment. Lately all she ever talks about is enviro-this and oxy-that. I can't pronounce the words, so please don't ask me what they mean.

"PLAYING BAT BOY AND SECOND BASE, TAAAAG ORTIZ!"

DeeBee's little brother makes me feel better for not knowing so much about astroball. He can hardly swing the bat. Okay, I know he's a lot younger than the rest of us. At least he tries.

"AT SHORTSTOP, MIIIIKO SAAAATO!"

It must help Miko to know karate. And besides, she can jump and flip all over the astroball field better than anybody else. Yeah, Miko is full of surprises. She's our best infielder. But she can't throw the astroball two meters.

"AND FINALLY, ON THE PITCHING MOUND TODAY, MIIIIR CHEKHOV!"

Please pronounce my name "MEER CHECK-off." There, that's better. Russian names are kinda hard to say. Now, pay attention, because I think I can do this. Maybe I won't pitch as fast as a drone, but teams don't use drones to pitch in real games, so who's checking?

Of course, other kids on the station tried out, too, in case you were wondering. Ben and Venus Mooney—they're brother and sister. Philly (short for Philadelphia) Photon and Alex Saturn were there, too. So were DeeBee's drone, MAC, and our talking dog, Zero-G. I think they thought they were going to be on the team, too.

No chance of that.

The only question was: Who would *really* make the team?

"All right!" Coach LaSolar's holo-picture finally blinked back on a few minutes later. "Listen up, and I'll tell you who's in. First of all, thanks to everybody who tried out. You did your best, and that's something."

Not in my case, I sighed. I couldn't hit an astroball if it orbited my nose.

Hey! Don't you dare tell anyone I said that.

"So, here's the roster." And he read us his list: Buzz, DeeBee, Miko, Tag . . .

No kidding? Tag too? This was getting to be an all-AstroKids team. Cool. Ben and Venus Mooney, Philly Photon, Alex Saturn . . .

"And . . ."

I held my breath.

"Vladimir Chekhov."

"Yeee-HAW!" Buzz whooped. He pounded me on the back. But then I saw the color drain from his face when he heard what Coach LaSolar said next.

"Chekhov will be the team captain."

CLEO-7 to Moon Base 02, come in, please. We're not reading you.

Me?

Captain?

Yikes!

I looked over at my mom, who gave me a double thumbs-up.

Now I was in trouble.

Big trouble.

Captain Mir in
4 Command

* * *

You understand why I was sweating. Me, captain of the *CLEO* Sevens? Yeah, right! I mean, don't get me wrong—I told Coach LaSolar I'd do it. But tell me why *I* should be captain, instead of Buzz?

My dad, that's why. Station Commander Chekhov. I found out he'd called Coach LaSolar. And when my dad calls people, well, you know. Station Commander Chekhov is spelled with a capital S and a capital C, remember.

So now I had to call practices? Tell people what to do? Lead the team? Act like a coach? I couldn't even play the game!

* * *

The next morning, I looked around the empty

rec-pod and blew my captain's hyperwhistle. *Tweeeee!*

"I say, Master Mir, do you mind?" Zero-G buried his ears under his paws.

"Sorry." I let the whistle drop around my neck. And I nearly tripped backward into DeeBee's bucket.

"What *is* that stuff?" I held my nose. You would have, too.

DeeBee looked up from where she was kneeling next to a big red plastic bucket on the floor. She sighed, as if telling me would spoil the secret.

"I'm growing a special bacteria in low-G conditions to see if it affects the molecular blah blah blah . . ."

Okay, so she didn't really say "blah blah blah." But that's as close as I can get to what DeeBee did say. All I know is, her bucket *reeked*. I think long-range scent scanners could probably pick it up all the way from Earth. "*CLEO*-7, Houston here. Something stinks up your way!"

"Looks like caterpillar *knug* to me," added Tag. That would be *gunk* in backward talk.

"Actually, I have taken samples from several

species of caterpillar . . ."

Yikes. So DeeBee was off in left field again with a nasty science experiment. Miko was practicing slo-mo karate moves. Tag was trying to teach Zero-G to fetch. Ben and Venus were playing with a 3-D Nin-12-do game, and Philly and Alex were late. Only MAC looked ready to practice, and he wasn't on the team.

I didn't have a clue what to do next.

Well, my dad always told me to "fake it till you make it." I don't know if that's the best advice, but now was my chance to try it.

I pulled out Mister e to see what a captain was supposed to do. Let's see: cape, capital, captain . . . Bingo!

"Okay." I took a deep breath, then peeked down at my e-reader to find out what to say. "I need the first officer to report."

Everybody stared at me blankly. Huh?

"Uh, Mir . . ." Buzz rubbed his chin. "I think you've got the wrong captain program going. You're our *team* captain, not a *ship* captain."

Well, I'm not brain dead. I *know* the difference between ship captains and astroball team captains.

It's just that—oh, bag it. So much for "fake it till you make it."

"Here, let me see that reader." MAC floated a little closer. He looked pretty goofy in a bright red *CLEO* Sevens hat. "I can update the memory files for you."

"Sure." I waved my hand. "Anything is better than what I have."

Better believe it. How was I supposed to be team captain with lousy mem files? That would be almost as bad as trying to hit an astroball with the sun in your eyes.

Click. Zvoooom. Click-click-click. MAC held a scanner next to the reader and did his data thing. I guess he added fresh info. He mumbled something to himself, like, "I'll show them who has the best mem files." *Click. Zvooom.* "When I get finished with this Mister e . . ."

He handed it back to me a minute later.

"Thanks." I took back Mister e and checked out the screen. The little guy was waving his hand, which gave me an idea. Okay. We could do that.

"Let's start, ah, throwing practice," I told

them. "We have only a couple of weeks before the tournament, you know."

Yeah. That sounded good. Throwing practice.

"Good call, captain! But can any of you throw?"

Grr. I didn't even want to turn around to look at Deeter Meteor, my best un-friend from *CLEO-5*.

"Why did they let you onto the station, Deeter?" I asked.

"Whoa! Down, boy." Deeter was in good form. "Me and my friends were just cruising around on our scooters, and we thought we'd pay you a visit."

"Scooters?" I looked around the rec-pod. "What scooters?"

That must have been their cue. *BAM!* Something thunked against the double-wide doors from the hallway. *Zvooop!* Three two-kid space scooters came busting into the rec-pod.

Deeter and his gang sure knew how to make a grand entrance.

"We just wanted to say hi, Chock-off!" Deeter grabbed his friend's passing scooter to hitch a

ride around the huge room. "We're being good neighbors. We wanted to see how your team was doing."

"Seen enough?" I stretched out my hands as the three scooters crisscrossed the room. Deeter svooped right over my head, then wheeled back around and nearly bowled me over.

"Gangway!" he yelled.

I had to step back to keep from getting run over.

But I didn't see DeeBee behind me. I waved my arms, but I couldn't stop my fall.

Seat first—right into DeeBee's stinky bug gunk.

5 Nickname Nutty ✳ ✳ ✳

Ka-SPLASH!

Oh man. Nyet, this was not pretty. I was taking a bath in DeeBee's dark green science soup, her caterpillar part stew.

I was thinking, *This is not good. Not good at all!*

"Are you okay, Mir?" Buzz was the first to give me his hand. Miko and DeeBee were right behind him.

"You ruined DeeBee's experiment!" Tag shouted.

That made Deeter and his gang laugh even harder.

"Yeah, Chock-off. You *ruined* it!" Deeter held his stomach, he was laughing so hard.

"He didn't ruin anything." Give DeeBee credit. She stomped her foot and turned on the

Meteor gang with star fire in her eyes. "And you boys had better leave."

"Whoa!" Deeter raised his hands, pretending to give up. "Does this mean you don't want to play a practice game?"

DeeBee stared him down, and nobody wins a stare down with DeeBee. Not even Deeter.

"Ah, you *CLEO* Sevens don't have a chance anyway," he finally mumbled.

"Oh yeah?" Tag wasn't going to let Deeter get away with that.

"Cool your jets, Tag." DeeBee held him back.

"Do you get the feeling we're not welcome here?" Deeter asked his buddies. They made another couple of loops in their space scooters, just over Venus's and Ben's heads. And with a war whoop, Deeter led the way through the doors. It's a wonder he didn't run anybody down. I heard them laughing down the hallways before the doors svooshed shut once more.

"All right," I found my voice as I tried to dry off with a few rags. DeeBee's bug stuff was sure stinky. "Let's get started."

"Are you kidding?" asked DeeBee. "After all that?"

"Thanks for helping me," I answered. If it was the last thing I ever did, I was going to make sure we beat Deeter and his gang in the tournament. "But we're not afraid of them."

"Say, that gives me an idea." Zero-G sniffed my soaking wet clothes. "I have an astroball nickname for you."

An astroball nickname?

"Of course," he went on. "Everyone needs an astroball nickname. And we're going to call you 'No Fear Mir.'"

"No Fear!" piped in Miko. "That's perfect."

Whatever. We needed to start our practice. But this tells you something about the *CLEO* Sevens: We spent the next hour figuring out nicknames.

No kidding. The next *hour*! You know, like Moose, Goose, Hippo, Hack, or Junior. No-Quit Schmit and Three-Finger McGee. If you play astroball, I guess you have to have a nickname.

"I want to be 'Ragtag,'" Tag told us.

Fine with me. And after twelve revotes, we

finally decided to call DeeBee "Professor," Buzz "Buzzsaw," and Miko "Magic Miko."

QUESTION 05:
   But don't the AstroKids already *have* nick-names?

ANSWER 05:
   Yeah, now you have three names to remember for each AstroKid. Like Theodore, Tag, and RagTag. Daphne (but don't call her that!), DeeBee, Professor. Lamar, Buzz, Buzzsaw. I guess you could say we like our nicknames here in space.

Oh man, I was ready to retire after just an hour. I tried to get Buzz to take the job. He'd know what to do.

"No, no." Buzz put up his hands. "You're doing great. And Coach LaSolar said—"

"I know what he said," I admitted. "But don't you want a turn, too?"

"Nah." Buzz, I mean Buzzsaw, shook his head. "You hit us a few balls, and we'll field 'em for you."

"Right." I could do that. Still, I checked with Mister e real quick to make sure I was doing the right thing.

"With your left hand, toss the ball straight up over your head," said my little sports expert. But this time, his bat looked weird. Round and flat at the end, with lots of crisscrossed strings. Huh? "Now hit it straight over the net."

Great advice, if you were playing weightless tennis. I hit the Reset button.

"Back again?" asked Mister e. "Okay, here. Hold the ball with both hands. Keep your eye on the sbasket."

The "sbasket"? What game were we playing now?

I looked for MAC to help me out. "MAC? Since you fixed the mem files, Mister e has been . . . well, all mixed up."

"Oh dear. Perhaps I should try to reload the files and—"

"Er, on second thought, maybe not right now. Thanks." I didn't want him making it worse! "Maybe it'll clear up."

And maybe it wouldn't. Mister e was still

mixed up, and I was on my own.

Forget tennis, I told myself. *Forget sbasketball.*

I tossed up the ball and took a swipe.

And another.

And another.

"Juice it, No Fear!" yelled DeeBee.

About ten swipes later . . .

WHACK!

Hey, how about that? Piece of cake! The astro-ball took off for the ceiling like a booster rocket.

Well, a booster rocket for a *small* spaceship.

Or maybe a booster rocket for a shopping cart.

"I've got it!" cried RagTag. He took three giant leaps, way up into the air, to get under the pop fly. It looped and swooped.

"I've got it!" yelled Buzzsaw. I don't think he heard RagTag.

"I've got it!" hollered the Professor. She didn't look where she was going, either.

You guessed what's coming.

Ker-THUNK!

That had to hurt.

Nep2nade C, 6 Anyone?

✳ ✳ ✳

I'll tell you something: When RagTag, Buzz-saw, and the Professor ran into each other at that practice . . .

Well, it wasn't the last time they messed up.

In fact, if you count all the times we dropped the ball . . .

Or if you count all the times we swung and missed . . .

And if you count all the times we just plain goofed up . . .

Okay, do me a favor: Please don't count.

Sample 01: Monday Practice

Me: "We're here at the *CLEO* Sevens' Practice Camp, folks, for another exciting morning of heads-up astroball. I'm Mir 'No Fear' Chekhov, along with my good friend Mister e. E?"

Mister e: "That's right, Mir. It looks as if these wrestlers need a little work if they're going to win in the Saturn League."

Me: (Puzzled pause.)

Okay, was it me, or did Mister e just start talking about wrestling? See, I thought we were supposed to be practicing astroball. Not Saturn League Wrestling.

Oh well. It seemed like every day we practiced, we got a little bit . . . worse. Coach LaSolar checked in with us like he did before. But what could he really do long distance?

Sample 02: Tuesday Practice

Me: "Hey, Tag, where's your sister? Practice was supposed to start fifteen minutes ago."

Tag: (Looking at his gripper shoes.) "Ah, well, DeeBee's kinda *ysub* right now."

Me: "Busy?" (Groaning.) "With what? How are we supposed to win if she's too busy to practice?"

Tag: (Still looking at his gripper shoes.)

"Well, I think she might have said something about her experiment, maybe."

Miko: (Stepping in to save the day.) "Don't worry, Mir. I can play catcher if you need someone."

Sample 03: Wednesday Practice

Coach LaSolar: "So how are the practices coming, Chekhov? Getting ready for the big day next week?"

Me: "Yes, sir." (If he only knew!)

Coach LaSolar: "How's batting practice coming?"

Me: "We're swinging the bats, sir." (Swinging was the right word.)

Coach LaSolar: "Good. Good to hear it."

Me: "Yes, sir. Lots of bats swinging." (Lots. *Whiff!*)

RagTag: (Whispering in the background.) "But did you tell him nobody's hitting, Mir?"

Me: "SHHHH!"

Coach LaSolar: "Eh? What's that?"

Me: "Nothing, sir. We'll see you soon."

There, you see? I was even beginning to think maybe Deeter Meteor had been right. Maybe the *CLEO* Sevens *didn't* have a chance to win the tourney.

But every time I thought that, I could have kicked myself.

"We can do this." I gritted my teeth and watched Magic Miko throw the ball *way* over DeeBee's head. Again.

"Yeah, we can do this." And I closed my eyes when RagTag tried to hit a *really* slow pitch. How long can a little guy spin so quickly a meter in the air?

"Whee!" yelled Tag. "This is fun!"

"I think it's just a matter of getting more strikes," said Mister e. He was still in my pocket, as usual. Maybe I hadn't heard him quite right.

"What are you talking about, *more* strikes?" I slipped out Mister e and stared at my mixed-up teacher. "This is astroball, or did you forget again? We *don't* want strikes."

"Oh no." Mister e smiled and held up a big purple-and-orange bowling ball. "Strikes are the best. Here, I'll show you. One holds the ball so,

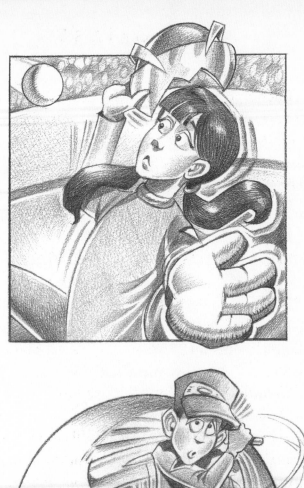

swings it underneath as one takes three steps down the lane, and—"

Ay! I hit the Reset button again.

"Who are you talking to, Mir?" Buzzsaw wanted to know. He slipped our flatbats and practice astroballs into a duffel bag. We were done for the day.

"Uh, er . . ." Quick! I slipped Mister e back into my pocket and turned around and looked like nothing was going on. No point in anyone knowing I still needed help learning the game. "Was I talking to someone?"

"Hmm." Buzzsaw shrugged. "See you at practice tomorrow."

✳ ✳ ✳

What was the use of practice? I asked myself that over and over when I holed up alone in our holo-room that night.

We're just going to go out there and look silly.

Click! I decided to forget it all and have fun watching a *real* astroball game. At least the pros didn't strike out.

"Deep Space Ten and the Moon Base 2 Apollos," I said as I settled into my dad's big easy chair.

"I knew that."

"What are *you* doing here?" I yelped and turned around. MAC had followed me home!

"Oh! Terribly sorry to startle you. I just came to ask again if I might fix your e-reader. I feel responsible. I can help."

As in, Mister e's problems were his fault. True, but I wasn't so sure MAC was the right repairman.

I turned back to the holo-vision set just in time to see a pro astroball player selling the latest space sports drink.

"Nep2nade C!" he grinned straight at me. "Beat your sports thirst so you can win! It's what the champions drink."

Champions, huh? Champions win. Losers lose. And if drinking Nep2nade C would help us win, then I'd be all for that.

It couldn't hurt, right?

"That's what we need!" I yelled and jumped out of the chair. MAC could hardly keep up with me as I ran to the digital food copier at the all-night snack counter.

"You can key in the Nep2nade C code, can't you?" I asked the drone. "You said you wanted to help."

"Yes, but first I should fix—"

"Please just do it!" I commanded him. "And make it double strong. No, triple strong! With extra vitamins."

Well, what's a drone supposed to do? I hoped no one saw us lugging the big red jug of Nep2nade C Sports Drink back to the rec-pod.

"Actually, let's keep it where it won't get lost," I told MAC. "We'll stash it with the other jugs in DeeBee's workshop."

"If you say so." He tried to balance the jug on his head like a lady in *Galaxy Geographic Magazine*, but I had to help him.

"And, MAC?"

"Yes, Master Mir?"

"Don't tell anybody about this, okay?"

"About a *sports drink*? It is only to keep you from getting thirsty, not a magic elixir."

I wasn't quite sure what an *elixir* was.

"I know that. But the *CLEO* Sevens need all the help we can get."

Boy, that was for sure!

7 Weird Wired　✳ ✳ ✳

Okay. Maybe the Nep2nade C would help, and maybe it wouldn't. I figured if we Sevens didn't worry about being thirsty, we'd be able to concentrate more on winning.

Or something like that.

What if it's just a bunch of hooey? I asked myself, back home in the Chekhov apartment. I flipped through five thousand holo-channels. The pro astroball game was over, and there wasn't anything good on. *Cooking With Chef Pluto* was a snooze. So was the infomercial about the amazing new "Just Move to Space" weight-loss program. I was still flipping when my dad finally came home from work.

"So, how's the team admiral?" he asked. The door zvooped shut behind him.

Was that a joke? With Dad, you couldn't be sure.

"Doing great." I didn't think he wanted to hear all about the *CLEO* Sevens. He was so busy with important stuff like running the space station. "We've been practicing."

"Yes, of course. And you teach them everything you know about this game, this astrobobble?"

"Sure, Dad." It wouldn't do any good to tell him what I *didn't* know. My father thought I knew *everything*. I could tell you what was coming next, though. A speech about the famous Chekhov family—my ancestors, the first space pioneers.

"The only thing more famous than Chekhov athletes are Chekhov pioneers, nyet? Space pioneers."

What did I tell you?

"In fact, did I ever tell you the story about your great-great-great . . . well, your ancestor Yuri Chekhov?"

"I think so, Dad."

"He was one of the first to orbit in the International Space Station, and . . ."

For the hundredth time, he told me the story about the old days, when the first space stations were being built. A hundred and seventy-five years ago. And how the brave Chekhovs—

"We Chekhovs, we find a way."

"I know. Say, I was wondering. Do you have to work this weekend?"

He gave me his "you must be an alien" look. "This weekend?"

"Right. This Saturday. Everybody's going to the tournament. I thought maybe you could stop by."

"Oh yes, Saturday. Well . . ." He cleared his throat. "I'm sorry, Mir. But I have a very, very important orbit test that day."

I tried not to let my face drop. After all, it wasn't the first time.

"Sure, Dad. No big deal. I was just thinking."

"You will holo-record it, won't you?"

I nodded.

"And your team will, of course, win?"

"Well . . ."

"Of course you will. Chekhovs always win."

He winked at me before he rushed off.

Right. *Chekhovs always win.* But how were we going to win this time? Would my idea really help?

Right. Like not being thirsty was really going to make a difference. I sighed. Want to know the truth? The more I thought about it, the lamer my Nep2nade C plan sounded.

"We'll find out," I muttered.

MAC came closer to hear what I was saying. Wait—MAC again?

"You're following me, aren't you?" I asked him.

MAC hovered about three inches from my face, blinking his green lights. I think that meant his bubble memory was working.

"Do you want me to tell you how to win the tournament?" he finally asked.

"More Nep2nade C?"

"No. Give me your e-reader and follow me, please."

He held out one of his hands.

I didn't budge. "Are you kidding? You already mixed up Mister e enough. I don't think—"

"No, no, Master Mir. This is different. This is ChampVision."

I almost bit my tongue. The silly drone had blown another circuit!

"ChampVision?"

"ChampVision. I will show you how to link your e-reader straight to your brainwaves."

That sounded weird . . . and a little dangerous. But I followed him to our practice room in the rec-pod.

"First, we hide the e-reader in your astroball hat."

"All right. But how do I watch it when it's under my hat?"

"You do not watch it."

"Then what good is it?"

"Let me make it simple for you. Step 01: Mister e hits a home run on the e-reader. Step 02: The e-reader sends a signal straight to your brain. Step 03: When your brain gets the message, your muscles do the same thing Mister e does. So, step 04—"

"I hit a home run, too!"

MAC's lights blinked like he was an over-loaded Christmas tree.

"I think you are getting the picture now."

Boy, was I. MAC rewired my e-reader, and we taped it inside my hat.

"Is it on?" I asked.

"Try it." MAC orbited my head, checking the hat to make sure the reader was safe inside. "Tell it what you want to do."

"Okay." I picked up a bat and an astroball. "Let's hit a home run."

Well, we didn't have a pitcher-drone handy. So I just had to toss up the ball and take a whack at it.

Ga-BOIIINGGG! For the first time in my life, I connected. I mean, *really* connected. You should have seen that astroball go!

BING! Off the ceiling.

BWANG-BWUNG! Off the walls.

THWATT! Off the floor, and back up.

"Hey!" I jumped up and down. "This thing really works! Let's try something else."

How about catching: Over the shoulder? Yep. Running and diving? No sweat. Throwing the ball? Straight down the middle! Strike three—you're out! I couldn't tell you how it worked. But it wasn't like I was a puppet on a string. It's just that when I swung the bat, my muscles seemed to know what to do. When I threw the ball, it went where it was supposed to. All of a sudden, everything was different. But I had a teeny, tiny question in the back of my mind.

Was this legal?

I was afraid to ask.

The tournament was only a few days away, remember. And I heard again what my dad had told me.

"Chekhovs always win."

With ChampVision, we couldn't lose.

8 Under Wraps ✳ ✳ ✳

Fast-forward a few days. You should have seen the rec-pod, all set up for the All-*CLEO* AstroBall Tournament. Somebody hung cool-looking banners all over the curved walls, and each field was fenced off by a purple force field curtain. All three fields were set up so three games could be played at once. By 0800 that morning, people were already beginning to fill up the floating bleachers.

Except my dad. I checked. Nyet, he wasn't there. He had said he couldn't make it, right? Anyway, he probably wouldn't have understood the game. Why would he want to watch his son's team win the All-*CLEO* AstroBall Tournament if he didn't understand the game?

Welcome to the Official Pre-Game Show!

"It's a pressure cooker out there, fans. A real nail biter. The crowd is going wild!"

"YAAAAAAYYY!"

(That's the sound of the crowd going wild.)

"Morning, folks, 'No Fear' Mir here with your play by play. Just remember two things as we start this match-up between the mighty *CLEO* Sevens and the so-so *CLEO* Threes. First, always root for the winner. That way, you won't ever be let down. And second, don't forget that most of the game is half mental."

Whatever. Forget announcing. This was the real thing. And when the other team bounced into the rec-pod, RagTag had to pick his jaw up off the deck and plug his eyeballs back in.

"Don't worry about 'em," I said.

"What are you grinning about, Mir?" Buzzsaw sized up the other team. "We're going to get creamed."

"Yeah," RagTag chimed in. "That guy's arms

are as big around as your legs. He can probably hit it from here to Pluto."

That was probably true. But I straightened my cap and told myself my teammates still didn't know about ChampVision. I hadn't shown it to anybody during practices, so this was going to be a surprise.

"One good thing about this tournament," Professor DeeBee told us as she did toe-touches and stretches. She was all decked out in her brand-new *CLEO* Sevens outfit, with the blue-and-red hat and matching sweats.

"What's that?" asked Magic Miko.

"We'll lose the first game, and it'll be all over."

"Yeah," agreed Ben and Venus, who usually said the same thing.

I had to grin. "Come on, you guys, have a little faith. And besides, guess what I got us?"

Everybody looked at me, except Philly and Alex, who were late again. This was the moment I had been waiting for.

"Escape pods to Earth?" RagTag asked.

"Nyet." I shook my head. "A big jug of Nep2nade C, drink of champions. MAC is fetching it for us right now."

"Hey, thanks a lot, Chock-off!"

Groan. Deeter again? I knew he would be there to play in the tourney, but . . .

We turned around to see him plant himself in front of MAC. DeeBee's drone was just coming in through the crowd, dragging the big red cooler jug.

"The best sports drink in the solar system, eh?" Deeter crowed. "What the champions drink."

"Pardon me," began MAC.

Deeter brushed him off. "Well, my team and I have been warming up all morning," he said. "And we're the only champions here. I'm sure you won't mind if we help ourselves."

What could I say? Deeter was not waiting for an okay. He just grabbed the jug from MAC and hitched it up on his shoulder, like a power weight lifter. Then he cranked open the faucet and took a big swig.

Sluuuurrp.

That was a very big gulp.

"Hey, don't slobber all over it." RagTag

stepped up to stop him.

Too late. Because just then, Deeter dropped the jug, gasped for air, gripped his neck, and gagged.

He rolled over on his back.

He squealed, huffed, and puffed.

His eyes bugged out like twin supernovas.

"*That* . . . was . . . Nep2nade . . . C?" gasped Deeter. Nuclear steam was hissing out his ears. "It tasted like . . ."

"Oh, *that's* my caterpillar bacteria." DeeBee dragged the red jug off to the side. "It's an experiment, Deeter. You really shouldn't have been drinking it."

"But . . . but . . ." Deeter's face turned almost as green as the caterpillar gunk. He started to crawl away to his own game.

"Terribly sorry, old man." MAC floated around Deeter, poking him with a finger or two. "I must have picked up the wrong jug. They were both in red coolers."

"You'll get yours," Deeter whispered back. "And when we're done playing you AstroKids, you're going to look worse than—"

BEENG-BONG! That was the buzzer signaling the first games to start.

"Forget about the Nep2nade C," I told my team. "I'm not thirsty anyway."

"Me neither." Buzz looked at the red cooler and shivered. "Not anymore."

But DeeBee stopped us. "Shouldn't we pray first?"

That was a good idea. But for a second, I wondered what God would think of ChampVision. Maybe it was a little, you know . . .

Sneaky.

"Lord, I know the other team is probably going to whomp us," DeeBee led the prayer for us all. "But I just pray that Deeter won't get sick."

Well, all right, I thought.

"And also that you'd help us to play today like a team is supposed to play."

Like a team is supposed to play?

Everybody said "amen" but me. After all, they still didn't know what I knew.

They didn't know about ChampVision.

⑨ Go, Sevens! ✳ ✳ ✳

You should have heard the crowd when they called our names. I'd never heard anything so loud. We were the hometown boys and girls, right?

"AND NOW," yelled the announcer. I don't think he needed the loudspeakers. "OUR VERY OWN *CLEEEEEO* Sev-ens!"

Here's the Play by Play

"Mir 'No Fear' Chekhov here, folks, bringing you the latest play by play. And I've got to tell you, the crowds are pumped up for this classic matchup between the hometown faves, the *CLEO* Sevens, and the upstart *CLEO* Threes. They're all wound up. They're jazzed. They're thrilled.

They're . . . Well, anyway, the Threes will take the field first."

(Polite applause.)

"And now, ladies and gentlemen, space travelers and lunar rovers, batting first for the Sevens, Magic Miko Saaaaato!"

"Woooop-woooooo! Yaaah! Yeeee! Yoooo!"

We all made as much noise as we could. Even Zero-G did backflips—remember things are close to weightless in the rec-pod—and howled. MAC put his hands together and made a metal crunching noise, which was his way of clapping.

Click-click, CRUNCH!

MAC doesn't realize quite how strong he is. I mean, he could hurt himself. I told him to cool it and try some other way of cheering.

Anyway, I could give you the blow by blow, play by play from now until the end of the series. We'll get to that, I promise. But for now, let me just tell you that tough little Magic Miko drew a lead-off walk.

I mean, the pitcher threw her four pitches that were too high or low to hit. Pretty good for us! A runner on first.

The Professor batted next. She hit the ball pretty well but right at third base. Whoops. Out number one.

Buzzsaw hit better, but the center fielder made a great twenty-foot diving catch. Diving catches look extra-cool when the catcher is almost weightless. Out number two.

And then it was me. I picked up my favorite bat, a shiny see-through sparkly one that Buzzsaw used, too.

"Home run to left field," I whispered.

I think the catcher from the other team heard me. "I don't think so, kid," he mumbled.

The pitcher wound up. But how could I miss? I went ahead and took the first swing.

Da-ZWOIIINGGG!

Back to the Play by Play

"Belted, deep to left. He's going back, back . . . Good-bye, astroball. My, oh my!"

Well, how about that! I trotted around those bases with the biggest grin you ever saw. Even bigger when I rounded third and looked up into the stands.

Everybody was screaming and yelling their heads off. DeeBee and Tag's folks were there; so were the Brights, Mr. and Mrs. Mooney, Philly Photon's mom, and Alex Saturn's folks, too. But right in the front row . . . I could hardly believe it.

"TOUCHDOWN!" yelled Dad.

My dad.

He held both his hands in the air.

Wrong sport. But so what?

Buzzsaw helped me to my feet.

"Watch out for that base," he told me. "It's easy to trip over."

I didn't care. I gave galaxy salutes to RagTag and the Professor and Magic Miko and Ben and Venus and Buzz. Philly and Alex, too. Then I jumped on home plate with both feet. Only, I jumped so hard I bounced back into the ceiling. And once you start spinning up there, it's sort of hard to stop.

But, like I said: SO WHAT?

"Hey, maybe we're not going to lose, after all!" Buzzsaw told me.

Are you kidding? We won that game 13–5, the next game 5–0, and the next game 6–1. Are you seeing a pattern here?

WHOOOSH. I was even pitching pretty good. Professor and I had worked out some signals for when she played catcher. One finger meant a fastball. Two a curve. And if she wiggled her little finger? That was a signal for the special No Fear Mir ball.

For that one, I would jump up about ten feet, hang there for a minute, and fire.

"That's the way!" my dad yelled after I fanned the last *CLEO-4* batter. Had he forgotten about his very important meeting?

Dad cupped his hands and yelled, "I told them to do the orbit test themselves!"

No kidding?

"This is more important," he hollered.

"This is in-CRED-ible!" Tag took a bow after we finished off *CLEO-1*, *CLEO-2*, *CLEO-3*, and *CLEO-4*. "I thought we were supposed to be bad."

Well, not anymore. The only other team that had been winning as much as us was ... you guessed it: Deeter Meteor and the *CLEO* Fives. Maybe there was something in that bug juice.

I was about to find out.

🔟 Time Out! ✳ ✳ ✳

Deeter and his gang weren't just winning. Anyone who played *CLEO-5* that day was demolished.

Pulverized.

Smashed.

Sliced and diced.

Taken to the cleaners.

Whomped.

Crushed.

Pounded.

Thrashed.

Can you think of any other way to say "beaten badly"?

Then fill in the blank here _____.

(Very good. Thank you.)

You get the idea. But hey, by the final game of the day, we were still feeling pretty good. A few bruises, a sore arm or two, but we were cruising in hyperdrive.

"After all," I told the team. "Four games, four wins. All we need is one more to win everything."

In other words, all we needed was to beat Deeter and the Fives.

"Yeah." RagTag stood on his head and crossed his arms in his best hall-of-fame pose. "We can take 'em. We're number one."

Were we? The first Five who stepped up to the plate looked as if he would chew me up and spit me out. He wiggled his black helmet, then set his helmet controls. Pretty cool. But did he have anything like ChampVision?

Don't think about it, I told myself. I didn't want to start feeling all guilty again. Not when we were doing so well.

"Master Mir!" MAC interrupted everything when he buzzed out to the mound. "You must call a time out."

"For what?" I didn't want Bruiser at the plate to get too hungry.

He glared at me and planted his size twenty sneakers.

"Comeonandpitchdaball!" growled Bruiser. That means "Please throw the ball my way, if you would be so kind. I would love to hit it into a thousand small metal pieces that will turn the outside air lock into a screen door. But only if you're ready."

Or something like that.

"Master Mir!" MAC buzzed even louder. "It is very important!"

Okay. I called a time out, and we all huddled by the pitcher's mound.

"So, what's so important?" I asked.

"It is your . . . it is your . . . hat!"

"What?" Buzzsaw didn't get it. Nobody else did, either.

"My hat's fine." A little heavy, but fine. I straightened it out. But when he said "hat," I knew he meant ChampVision. Our secret weapon.

"No, you do not understand." MAC was making me nervous. "I just found out you do not have any batteries."

"Can somebody tell me what he's talking about?" Professor DeeBee chewed her Galaxy Goop Gum and made a nice *pop* when she slapped her fist into her bright green glove.

"Long enough!" growled Bruiser.

"Hold on!" I raised my hand. And then I turned to MAC once more. "What do you *mean*, I don't have any batteries? We've been winning, haven't we?"

By this time, Professor was getting suspicious. You know, like she was figuring it out.

"Batteries? Winning?" she asked.

"All right, look." We didn't have much time left. But I tipped off my hat and pointed to the empty battery compartment in the ChampVision unit inside my hat. "There, see? No . . ."

". . . batteries."

And then I realized what that meant.

No batteries meant no power. No power meant no ChampVision. And no ChampVision meant . . .

"The batteries were missing from the start," said MAC. "All this time, you have been doing everything yourself!"

"Well, sure he has." RagTag still didn't get it. "He's hit three home runs, and . . ."

"What's that?" asked the Professor, looking at the hat.

I didn't have time to explain. So MAC slipped a couple of tiny new lithium battery disks into the unit, and it powered up with a blinking orange light. Next, he touched the cover and melted it in place.

"What did you do that for?" I asked.

"So they cannot fall out."

"Play ball!" yelled the drone-ump.

"Yes, sir," I yelled back. I grabbed the astroball and tried to stare down the hitter, the way I'd been doing all day. But this time, my head felt like it was spinning. Probably from the Champ-Vision—now turned on for the first time.

"Okay," I whispered. I hoped the Champ-Vision sensors would pick up my voice command for real this time.

"Strike," I whispered. "Strike."

The next part is tricky to explain. I didn't *have* to do what I did. It's just that the ChampVision made it so easy. And when I started moving, it seemed like the right thing to do.

And so when I wound up for the first pitch,

something funny happened. Instead of throwing it *over*hand, like any good astroball pitcher would do, I rolled it *under*hand, like a bowler.

A perfect strike! Except, this was a *bowling* strike, not an astroball strike.

Yikes! I heard the little voice in my hat saying, "A strike is when you knock down all ten pins in your first try."

I don't know about all ten pins, but I was going to knock Bruiser off his feet, easy. He jumped—but not high enough.

11 Fives to the Plate ✳ ✳ ✳

THUNK! You know the Bible story of how Goliath fell. Well . . . Bruiser made a pretty good Goliath.

"What's going on, Mir?" DeeBee trotted out to the mound. How could I tell her?

Nyet, I didn't know myself why ChampVision was going wacko. In the next few innings, I managed to make two free throws, a field goal, a touchdown, a slap shot, a hole in one, and a hat trick. Can you think of any sport I didn't cover?

The weird thing was, my dad didn't know the difference. He just kept clapping and smiling and cheering from the bleachers. He even cheered when I caught the ball and kicked it to our first baseman to make a soccer-style double play.

"I should have spent more time with you kids." In between innings, Coach LaSolar scratched his bald head. "I've never seen anything like this in my life."

Well, neither had anyone on the rest of the team. But we hung in there. And when the Fives scored a couple of runs, we scored a couple, too. So the astroball game was tied. But Deeter and his buddies were howling when I came up to bat in the last inning.

"You can do it, Mir," said Buzzsaw from behind me. We needed just one run to slip ahead.

"Get a hit," I whispered. "Get a hit."

To tell you the truth, I'd thought about switching off ChampVision. But how could I? You remember how MAC sealed in the batteries. Thanks to that, the On-Off switch had stopped working. And besides, I figured we still had a chance with it on. Maybe Mister e would still come through.

Anyway, the lanky Fives pitcher was already winding up for one of his warp-drive pitches.

"Hey, Mir!" Deeter yelled from his spot on first base. "Why don't you show us some ballet moves? You've done everything else."

What? I was in the middle of my swing before

I figured out what he'd said. But by then, it was too late.

Now I was in trouble. Big trouble.

"Don't listen to him," I told my hat. "Cancel! Cancel!"

Too late. All I could do was swat at the pitch and run.

ZVAAP! I hit it. The astroball dribbled down the third-base line, where Edwina Orbitt stooped to scoop it up. Maybe if I hurried, I could make it to first.

But that's when I heard Mister e's funny little voice telling me that "the most graceful move in ballet is the pirouette."

That's *peer-oo-ETT*, in case you were wondering. And in case you were wondering what a pirouette looks like, you should have been there. I pirouetted three times on my way to first base. Each time, about ten feet off the floor.

"Hands stretched out like a swan's wings," said Mister e.

Got it.

"Point your toes!"

I did that, too. Believe me, that's not easy to

do with astroball shoes on.

And hey, I almost made it to first base. The Fives were laughing so hard Edwina almost couldn't throw it to Deeter. I was out by a step.

But that was it. I'd had it. Bag this Champ-Vision.

"That does it!" Before I could change my mind, I tore my hat off and threw it on the Astro-turf.

Hard.

"Ouch." Mister e didn't like that. "What are you doing, Mir?"

"Tell me how to stomp grapes."

"Well, first take off your shoes . . ."

I would have stomped all over that hat, except MAC came to the rescue. He svooped in and picked up my hat before anyone else could figure out what was going on.

"We can fix ChampVision, Master Mir. I know how to do this." And MAC whisked back to the dugout before I could grab my hat back.

That left me without my hat.

Without my ChampVision.

On my own.

Okay, I know I was on my own before, but that was different. I mean, then I had *thought* the ChampVision was on. Now that I knew the truth, well, it was more scary.

"I'm through," I told my team. "I'm sorry. I shouldn't have done it. It was a really lame idea."

"Hey, don't sweat it," Buzzsaw told me. Good old Buzz. But he didn't know what I was talking about. "We're in this together, remember?"

"Yeah, but how about we save the ballet for later?" said DeeBee. Now that we had a chance, she wanted to win this thing. I didn't blame her.

We were just three outs away from our big chance.

Final Inning
12 Surprise

✳ ✳ ✳

"You sure you guys don't want some more Nep2nade C?" RagTag yelled at the Fives from his place in the outfield. He did three flips. "We've got plenty more."

"I'll bet you do!" Deeter yelled back from the floating bench where he sat with his teammates. "Keep it."

"Batter up!" announced the drone-ump. It was the Fives' final turn to bat.

Okay, this was it. Just us and the Fives.

No thirst-quenching, refreshing Nep2nade C.

No help from Mister e.

And no ChampVision.

Could we still win?

Well, come to think of it, we probably should have been disqualified. Kicked out of the game for cheating.

My cheating. If you call bowling strikes and ballet dancing to first base cheating.

Of course, I had thought we were cheating the first four games, too. I guess we weren't, but I *thought* we were. I had been *trying* to cheat, and thinking about it made me feel pretty rotten. Trying to cheat was just as bad as really cheating, I guessed.

And I guessed I had plenty of 'fessing up to do.

But the truth is, we hadn't won those first four games because of ChampVision. And we hadn't won those first four games because I was such a hot player.

Nyet, we won those first four games because all of us were doing our part. I threw, DeeBee caught. Buzzsaw made a bunch of hits. RagTag ran his heart out, and Magic Miko made great plays. So had Ben and Venus out in the field. Philly and Alex, too.

And remember DeeBee's prayer back at the end of chapter 8? I'll wait while you flip back there to check it out. (Flip, flip, flip.)

Back already? So you remember now that she

didn't pray to win or to have the other teams lose. She prayed we'd play like a team, no matter who won or lost. And that's just what we were doing now.

"Time out!" I shouted. I'd almost forgot. I couldn't play astroball without a *CLEO* Sevens hat. I bounced back to our floating bench. And who do you think was waiting there?

"Dad!"

"Looking for this?" He held out my old hat to me.

Uh-oh. I couldn't put that thing back on my head. But when I took it, I noticed something different.

The ChampVision was gone.

Did Dad know?

"I'm proud of you, Mir."

"You are?"

"And not because your dancing reminded me of the Bolshoi Ballet back home in Moscow."

"Oh, that."

The Bolshoi is famous for dancers in funny tights who don't get dizzy when they twirl. I was hoping everybody would forget about *my* ballet, though.

"No, it was quite good. I didn't know astroball had ballet in it, but I liked it. Makes the game more interesting."

"Thanks, Dad, but I'm really sorry—"

"We can talk about it later." Yeah, he had to know about the ChampVision. "But don't forget I'm proud of you, win or lose."

That was a cool thing for my dad to say. Win or lose, huh? Well, with the next few pitches I was going to make sure it was *win*. I popped my hat back on my head. It felt better, lighter, and so did I. I climbed back on the mound for my last three outs.

"All we have to do is hold 'em," DeeBee told me. True. We were still tied. If we could hold them, we'd have another chance. But it wasn't going to be easy. The heart of the Fives' lineup was up next.

Edwina Orbitt.

Good old Bruiser.

And Deeter himself.

What did you expect? I took a deep breath

and checked DeeBee's signal. Fastball on the outside corner. Okay.

Craack! Edwina knocked my first pitch for a loop. Alex twirled and caught up to it, but only after it had bounced a couple of times. He made a sweet relay throw to second, but Edwina was too fast.

"SAFE!" cried the drone-ump.

"That's okay!" I yelled out to the others. "Next time."

But next time, Bruiser took a shot at my best curve ball. He whiffed a couple times, then finally caught it with the tip of his bat.

Buzz had to dive to his right to catch up with the wobbly hit. He flew through the air sideways like a rocket, but that left first base unguarded. So it was my job to run over there and catch the throw from Buzz, where I stepped on the bag before Bruiser could.

"OUT!" shouted the drone-ump.

"Yesssss!" yelled Miko and DeeBee. "Teamwork!"

"Better than the Bolshoi!" yelled Dad.

"Hole in one!" added Mom.

I held up my hand and tried to keep it all inside. One down, two to go. The crowd was going wild, for sure.

Professor DeeBee crouched down behind the plate and wiggled the pinkie of her free hand. That was the signal for my special No Fear Mir ball, remember?

Okay. I took a deep breath, flew up as high as I could, and let it fly.

Wheeeeeez . . .

CRAAACK!

By now, you know the sound of an astroball home run. And Deeter nailed it off the far wall. *Boinnng! Bwaaang!* and all the rest of it. It was gone.

And off the best pitch I could throw! All the *CLEO-5* fans came rushing and bouncing onto the field, screaming and hooting up an ion storm.

Final score: *CLEO* Fives 6, *CLEO* Sevens 4.

The rest of us, well, for a minute we stood there, frozen. I was afraid to look at anyone else.

But I was team captain, remember. I had one more job to do. I trotted up to Deeter and his

gang, my hand out. I was betting he would spit on it.

"Remind me never to go bowling with you, Chock-off," he said as a couple of his buddies lifted him to their shoulders. "You're dangerous. But you're okay."

And he slapped my hand with a spit-free high five.

"Anyone for some Nep2nade C?" RagTag came out with a jug and a bunch of cups.

"You're kidding, right?" Even DeeBee didn't look sure. Ben and Venus turned pale.

"Good job, *CLEO* Sevens!" MAC came buzzing up to us. "By my calculations, you ended up with the low score!"

"Which is good in golf and . . . and golf," I told him. "But not in astroball."

His green lights blinked a couple of seconds.

"I knew that, of course."

Of course.

It felt good to laugh. And honestly? I'd wanted to win, bad. We all did. No doubt about it. But then I looked over at my folks giving us a standing ovation. My dad gave me a big galactic thumbs-up. And it hit me.

Maybe I *had* won, after all.

Real Space Debrief

✳ ✳ ✳

Robots, Robots

Picture this: You're a scientist on the International Space Station—the *real* one—just doing your job. You need some more info for your weightless plant experiment, so you turn to a floating drone about the size of a softball. It's crammed with computers, cameras, sensors . . . even a small video screen.

You get the numbers you need from this little helper. And its camera looks over your shoulder to show scientists back on Earth what you're doing.

Sound like the far future, like something out of an ASTROKIDS story?

Maybe not. Right now, scientists are really

working on these tiny drones. Only, they call them PSAs, or Personal Satellite Assistants. Pretty soon, PSAs will help astronauts do their jobs better by

- giving them information, like a floating encyclopedia;
- acting like a station messenger;
- "sniffing" the air to make sure it's okay to breathe;
- showing what's up with an on-board camera. (Remember the Remote-Float Eyeball Cam in *About-Face Space Race*? It will work kind of like that.)

These drones will be perfect to send into places where it may be too dangerous for astronauts to go. Pushed by little fans, they'll float around using their sensors. Those sensors will tell them if there are any dangerous gases in the air, how warm it is, or what the air pressure is. Knowing that kind of stuff is a matter of life or death when you live up in space. After all, you can't just step outside for a breath of fresh air.

But you know what's really cool about the

NASA droids? The scientist who invented them got the idea from a story! It's a fact. Yuri Gawdiak came up with the idea, and he now heads up the drone-building project for NASA. He said part of the idea came from the *Star Wars* light-saber training droids. In the movie, softball-sized droids floated around and helped train the story's main characters in saber-fighting skills.

It just goes to show that made-up stories can lead to real-life science! So go ahead and dream. Use your God-given imagination. Because when you do and you leave the results to God, who knows? You might come up with an idea as cool as Yuri's. Maybe something that can help save lives, like NASA's PSAs.

Or maybe something like the robots that Earth police use to unplug bombs. They get close when people can't. Or the robots that help find sunken treasures and ships in deep-sea places people can't go. Robots are exploring other planets, and our own!

If you're really into it, you can join a robotics club, where people build robots for fun. You can enter the Robot Games or go to a robot store.

You can watch robot races on TV. Or you can even buy a robot dog called Aibo that understands more than fifty commands and can learn its own name. Better go to the bank first, though. That puppy costs a cool $1,500!

Call them drones, droids, or just plain robots. Any way you look at them, these high-tech gizmos are getting cooler and more amazing every day.

Fun Web sites to check out:

- How robots are being built for the International Space Station
  http://science.nasa.gov/headlines/y2001/ast23jul_1.htm?list113162
- Short movies on the ISS droid
  http://ic.arc.nasa.gov/ic/projects/psa—click on "simulation"
- Science fiction becomes science fact
  http://vesuvius.jsc.nasa.gov/er/seh/exhibit.html
- Very cool robot stuff for sale
  http://robotstore.com/links.asp

And the Coded Message Is...

✳ ✳ ✳

You think this AstroKids adventure is over? Nyet! Here's the plan: We'll give you the directions, you find the words. Write them all on a piece of paper. They form a secret message that has to do with *AstroBall Free-4-All*. If you think you got it right, log on to *www.bethanyhouse.com* and follow the instructions there. You'll receive free AstroKids wallpaper for your computer and a sneak peek at the next AstroKids adventure. It's that simple!

WORD 1:
chapter 10, paragraph 22, word 20 _____

WORD 2:
chapter 8, paragraph 3, word 14 _____

WORD 3:
chapter 4, paragraph 7, word 1 _____

WORD 4:
chapter 6, paragraph 34, word 25 _____

WORD 5:
chapter 2, paragraph 10, word 15 _____

WORD 6:
chapter 11, paragraph 15, word 3 _____

WORD 7:
chapter 3, paragraph 13, word 27 _____

WRITE IT ALL HERE:

_____

_____

(Hint: Chekhov, or rather, check out Colossians 3 in the Bible!)

Contact Us!   ✴ ✴ ✴

If you have any questions for the author or would just like to say hi, feel free to contact him at Bethany House Publishers, 11400 Hampshire Avenue South, Bloomington, MN 55438, United States of America, EARTH. Please include a self-addressed, stamped envelope if you'd like a reply. Or log on to Robert's intergalactic Web site at *www.elmerbooks.org*.

Launch Countdown

AstroKids 09:
Mid-Air Zillionaire

Miko Sato was afraid this day would come. The Apollo Children's Home has finally caught up with the one-time stowaway. When the AstroKids see an urgent message from the home's chairman, a zillionaire developer, they know this is no false alarm. He's coming to take her back!

Miko's friends want to help her. First, they find a place to hide her, and then they form the MPF, the Miko Protection Force. And that's nothing compared to DeeBee's FaceLifter, which helps change Miko's face to look like someone else's—when it's working, that is!

But not even the MPF can stop the chairman

from coming face-to-face with Miko. And Miko is in for the surprise of her life: She's inherited an entire asteroid! Will she trade her friends and life on *CLEO-7* for riches?